The THREE SILLIES

Illustrated by
Arthur Friedman

Troll Associates

Library of Congress Cataloging in Publication Data
Main entry under title:

The three sillies.

SUMMARY: A young man believes his sweetheart and her family are the silliest people in the world until he meets three others who are even sillier.
[1. Folklore—England] I. Friedman, Arthur, 1935-
PZ8.1.T384   398.2'2'0942   80-27636
ISBN 0-89375-486-2 (case)
ISBN 0-89375-487-0 (pbk.)

Copyright © 1981 by Troll Associates, Mahwah, New Jersey
All rights reserved. No part of this book may be used or reproduced in any manner whatsoever without written permission from the publisher. Printed in the United States of America.

10 9 8 7 6 5 4

The THREE SILLIES

Once upon a time, there lived a woodcutter who had a wife and a daughter. Now the girl was old enough to marry, but she had not yet found a man who would suit her. Finally, a suitable young man came to call.

"He is handsome," thought the girl, "and he seems quite clever." And so he was invited to stay for dinner.

When the roast was ready, the girl went down to the cellar to get some cider. She pulled a stool up in front of the cider barrel and sat down. She put a pitcher on the floor under the spout and turned the handle on. Then, to keep herself busy while the pitcher was filling, she let her eyes wander about the cellar. A heavy axe was stuck in one of the beams of the ceiling, and she gazed up at it.

"Oh, dear," she thought. "Suppose I should marry that young man upstairs, and we should have a child. And suppose our little child were to come down here to get some cider. And suppose that heavy axe fell down from the ceiling and landed on the child's head. That would be terrible!" So she began to cry. She cried so hard that she forgot all about the cider, which filled the pitcher and overflowed onto the floor.

After a time, the girl's mother began to wonder why her daughter had not returned with the cider. So she went down to the cellar and found her crying in front of the cider barrel. "Why do you sit there while the cider overflows from the pitcher?" asked the mother.

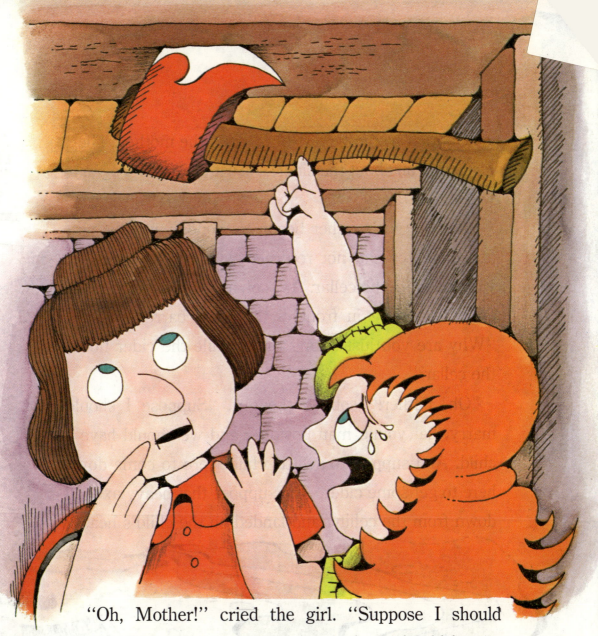

"Oh, Mother!" cried the girl. "Suppose I should marry that young man upstairs, and we should have a child. And suppose our little child were to come down here to get some cider. And suppose that heavy axe fell down from the ceiling and landed on the child's head!"

"Oh, that would be terrible!" cried the mother. Then, forgetting all about the cider, she sat down and began to weep.

Soon the girl's father began to wonder why his wife and daughter had not returned with the cider. So he went down to the cellar. As soon as he saw his wife and daughter sitting in front of the cider barrel, he said, "Why are you just sitting there while the cider floods the cellar?"

"Oh, Father!" sobbed the girl. "Suppose I should marry that young man upstairs, and we should have a child. And suppose our little child were to come down here to get some cider. And suppose that heavy axe fell down from the ceiling and landed on the child's head!"

"Oh, that would be terrible, indeed," cried the father. Then, forgetting all about the cider, he sat down and began to weep.

Upstairs, the young man was growing more and more thirsty. Finally, he decided to get the cider himself. So he went down the steps into the cellar. What a sight he saw! The floor was flooded with cider, and there sat the woodcutter and his wife and his daughter. Their heads were in their hands, and tears were in their eyes.

The young man quickly reached for the cider barrel and turned the spout off. "Whatever is the matter?" he asked. And when the girl told him, he laughed until his sides began to ache.

"Oh, you sillies!" he laughed. "In all my travels, I have never seen three bigger sillies than you!" Then he took the axe down and gave it to the woodcutter, saying, "I will marry your daughter only if I can find three bigger sillies than you!" And he went up the stairs and out the door.

Before long, he came to a stranger who was trying to teach a pig to climb an oak tree. "Why are you doing that?" asked the young man.

"The tree is full of acorns," replied the stranger. "If only my pig could get into the tree, he would have a real feast!"

"Why don't *you* climb the tree," suggested the young man. "Then you could just drop the acorns down to your pig."

"I never thought of that!" exclaimed the stranger.

"Oh, you silly!" laughed the young man. Then he continued down the road, thinking, "Well, I have found one big silly already!"

By nightfall, he had come to an inn. All the rooms were taken, so he had to share a room with another traveler. In the morning, he awoke to a terrible noise. The other traveler had hung his trousers up on the knobs of the dresser. He was trying to jump into them. Time after time, he ran across the room, and leaped into the air, trying to get both legs into his trousers at once. Sometimes he landed on the dresser. Sometimes he got tangled in the trousers. But most of the time, he landed on the floor with a bump and a thump.

Finally, the young man said, "Why don't you do it this way?" And he showed him how to hold his trousers in his hands and pull on first one leg, and then the other.

"That is a marvelous idea," said the traveler. "It will save me hours of work every morning!"

"You are a big silly!" said the young man. "And that makes two big sillies that I have found." Then he left the inn and started down the road.

Before long, he came to a small cottage that had grass growing on the roof. A ladder led from the ground to the roof, and an old woman was pushing a cow up the ladder. The cow did not want to climb the ladder, so it kept mooing and trying to get back down.

The young man watched for a few minutes. Then he asked, "Why in the world are you pushing your cow up the ladder?"

"The cow is hungry," explained the woman. "If I can just get her up this ladder, she can eat all that tender grass on the roof!"

"But the roof is too steep!" exclaimed the young man. "The cow will slip and fall off!"

"I will tie one end of a rope around her," replied the old woman. "I will drop the other end of the rope down the chimney, and fasten it to something. Then, even if the cow slips, she will not fall off."

But when she looked around the kitchen for something to fasten the rope to, she could not find anything large enough. "I guess I will tie it around myself," she said.

"Oh, you big silly," cried the young man. "That will never work!" But the woman would not listen. Suddenly, the cow slipped and fell off the edge of the roof. Down, down, down the cow fell. Up, up, up went the old woman, right into the chimney!

"Well," said the young man. "That makes three big sillies!"

So he returned to the woodcutter's house and said, "I have found three people who are even sillier than you. So now, I will marry your daughter." And because he did, some people think he was the biggest silly of all.

What do you think?